MW01017576

Edited by Belinda Gallagher
Designed by Oxprint Ltd

ISBN 0 86112 765 X
© Brimax Books Ltd 1991. All rights reserved.
Published by Brimax Books Ltd, Newmarket, England 1991.
Second printing 1992.
Printed in Hong Kong.

My First Book of
NURSERY RHYMES

Illustrated by Pamela Storey

Brimax • Newmarket • England

Hickory, Dickory Dock

Hickory, dickory dock,
The mouse ran up the clock;
The clock struck one,
The mouse ran down,
Hickory, dickory dock.

Jack and Jill

Jack and Jill went up the hill
To fetch a pail of water;
Jack fell down and broke his crown
And Jill came tumbling after.

Up Jack got and home did trot
As fast as he could caper;
He went to bed to mend his head
With vinegar and brown paper.

One, Two, Buckle my Shoe

One, two,
Buckle my shoe;
Three, four,
Knock at the door;
Five, six,
Pick up sticks;
Seven, eight,
Lay them straight;
Nine, ten,
A big fat hen;

Eleven, twelve,
Dig and delve;
Thirteen, fourteen,
Maids a-courting;
Fifteen, sixteen,
Maids in the kitchen;
Seventeen, eighteen,
Maids in waiting;
Nineteen, twenty,
My plate's empty.

Little Bo-Peep

Little Bo-Peep has lost her sheep
And can't tell where to find them;
Leave them alone, and they'll come home
And bring their tails behind them.

Little Bo-Peep fell fast asleep
And dreamt she heard them bleating;
But when she awoke, she found it a joke
For they were all still fleeting.

Then up she took her little crook,

Determined for to find them;

She found them indeed, but it made her heart bleed,

For they'd left their tails behind them.

It happened one day, as Bo-Peep did stray
Into a meadow hard by,
There she espied their tails side by side,
All hung on a tree to dry.

She heaved a sigh and wiped her eye
And over the hillocks went rambling;
And tried what she could, as a shepherdess should
To tack again each to its lambkin.

Humpty Dumpty

Humpty Dumpty sat on a wall,
Humpty Dumpty had a great fall;
All the King's horses
And all the King's men
Couldn't put Humpty together again.

Old King Cole

Old King Cole
Was a merry old soul,
And a merry old soul was he;
He called for his pipe,
And he called for his bowl,
And he called for his fiddlers three.

Every fiddler, he had a fiddle,

And a very fine fiddle had he,

Twee tweedle dee, tweedle dee, went the fiddlers;

Oh, there's none so rare

As can compare

With King Cole and his fiddlers three.

Boys and Girls Come Out to Play

Boys and girls come out to play,

The moon doth shine as bright as day.

Leave your supper and leave your sleep,

And join your playfellows in the street.

Come with a whoop and come with a call,

Come with a goodwill or not at all.

Up the ladder and down the wall,

A half-penny loaf shall serve us all.

You find milk and I'll find flour,

And we'll have a pudding in half an hour.

Little Miss Muffet

Little Miss Muffet
Sat on a tuffet,
Eating her curds and whey;
There came a big spider
Who sat down beside her
And frightened Miss Muffet away.

The Queen of Hearts

The Queen of Hearts
She made some tarts,
All on a summer's day;
The Knave of Hearts
He stole the tarts,
And took them clean away.

The King of Hearts
Called for the tarts,
And beat the Knave full sore;
The Knave of Hearts
Brought back the tarts
And vowed he'd steal no more.

Three Little Kittens

Three little kittens they lost their mittens,

And they began to cry,

Oh, Mother dear, we sadly fear

That we have lost our mittens.

What! Lost your mittens, you naughty kittens!

Then you shall have no pie.

Mee-ow, mee-ow, mee-ow,

No, you shall have no pie.

The three little kittens they found their mittens,

And they began to cry,

Oh, Mother dear, see here, see here,

For we have found our mittens.

Put on your mittens, you silly kittens,

And you shall have some pie.

Purr-r, purr-r, purr-r,

Oh, let us have some pie.

The three little kittens put on their mittens,

And soon ate up the pie;

Oh, Mother dear, we greatly fear

That we have soiled our mittens.

What! Soiled your mittens, you naughty kittens!

Then they began to sigh,

Mee-ow, mee-ow, mee-ow,

Then they began to sigh.

The three little kittens, they washed their mittens,

And hung them out to dry;

Oh, Mother dear, do you not hear

That we have washed our mittens?

What! Washed your mittens, then you're good kittens,

But I smell a rat close by.

Mee-ow, mee-ow, mee-ow,

We smell a rat close by.

One, Two, Three, Four, Five

One, two, three, four, five,
Once I caught a fish alive;
Six, seven, eight, nine, ten,
Then I let it go again.

Why did you let it go?
Because it bit my finger so;
Which finger did it bite?
This little finger on the right.

28

Pat-a-Cake, Pat-a-Cake

Pat-a-cake, pat-a-cake baker's man,
Bake me a cake as fast as you can;
Pat it and prick it, and mark it with B,
Put it in the oven for baby and me.

Baa, Baa, Black Sheep

Baa, baa, black sheep,
Have you any wool?
Yes sir, yes sir,
Three bags full;
One for the master,
And one for the dame,
And one for the little boy
Who lives down the lane.

Wee Willie Winkie

Wee Willie Winkie runs through the town,
Upstairs and downstairs in his nightgown;
Rapping at the window, crying through the lock,
Are the children all in bed, for now it's eight o'clock?

Sing a Song of Sixpence

Sing a song of sixpence,
A pocket full of rye;
Four and twenty blackbirds
Baked in a pie.

When the pie was opened
The birds began to sing;
Was not that a dainty dish
To put before the King?

The King was in his counting house,
Counting all his money;
The Queen was in the parlour,
Eating bread and honey.

The maid was in the garden,
Hanging out the clothes,
There came a little blackbird
And snapped off her nose.

Little Boy Blue

Little Boy Blue,
Come blow your horn,
The sheep's in the meadow,
The cow's in the corn;
But where is the boy
Who looks after the sheep?
He's under a haystack,
Fast asleep.
Will you wake him?
No, not I,
For if I do
He's sure to cry.

Hey Diddle Diddle

Hey diddle diddle,

The cat and the fiddle,

The cow jumped over the moon;

The little dog laughed

To see such sport,

And the dish ran away with the spoon.

Mary had a Little Lamb

Mary had a little lamb,
Its fleece was white as snow;
And everywhere that Mary went
The lamb was sure to go.

It followed her to school one day,
That was against the rule;
It made the children laugh and play
To see a lamb at school.

And so the teacher turned it out,
But still it lingered near,
And waited patiently about
'Til Mary did appear.

Why does the lamb love Mary so?
The eager children cry;
Why Mary loves the lamb, you know,
The teacher did reply.

Polly put the Kettle on

Polly put the kettle on,
Polly put the kettle on,
Polly put the kettle on,
We'll all have tea.

Sukey take it off again,
Sukey take it off again,
Sukey take it off again,
They've all gone away.

I See the Moon

I see the moon
And the moon sees me;
God bless the moon
And God bless me.